This book belongs to

Victoria Hislop

Maria's Island

Illustrated by Gill Smith

With thanks to Iro Porgiazidou for planting the little seed – V.H.

For my mum and dad – G.S.

First published 2021 by Walker Books Ltd
87 Vauxhall Walk, London SE11 5HJ

2 4 6 8 10 9 7 5 3 1

Text © 2021 Victoria Hislop
Illustrations © 2021 Gill Smith
The right of Victoria Hislop and Gill Smith to be identified as author and
illustrator respectively of this work has been asserted by them in accordance
with the Copyright, Designs and Patents Act 1988

This book has been typeset in Quercus
Printed in Italy

British Library Cataloguing in Publication Data:
a catalogue record for this book is available from the British Library
ISBN 978-1-4063-9907-3
www.walker.co.uk

WALKER
BOOKS

For my *vaftistira*, my god-daughter,

Loraini Skoulikari

My name is Rita. I live in London but I am half-Greek. Every summer I go with my parents on a long journey by plane and boat to the island of Crete to visit my yiayia (that's Greek for grandma). We stay in Agios Nikolaos in her apartment overlooking the sea and every afternoon we go to the beach to swim then come back in the evening to eat a lovely meal that Yiayia has cooked for us. She spends all day preparing it. Some evenings, we move the furniture and Yiayia puts on a record and teaches me steps from a Cretan dance. She has also taught me the Greek alphabet and I know lots of words now. She always calls me "agapi mou", which means "darling".

I sleep in Yiayia's room, and my parents are on a sofa that opens out to make a bed.

This morning, I overhear my mum asking her if she will come and live with us in England.

"It's too cold for me there," Yiayia replies. "And I have too much to look after here."

I know what she means about it being too cold, but I don't understand what she has to "look after" as she doesn't have any pets, just a few plants on her roof terrace.

It's almost the end of the holiday now and my parents have left for a trip to explore the other end of Crete and will be gone for two nights. I am very happy because it is the first time ever that I am staying on my own with Yiayia. I love her a lot and she is very fond of me too.

She is kind and gentle, with twinkly brown eyes and silver hair tied up in a bun. She is always in a flowery dress and never without an apron, because there's always something going in or coming out of the oven.

First thing in the morning, we start mixing sugar and flour to make my favourite biscuits. While they are baking, Yiayia gives me her old set of paints and I do a picture of the view from the balcony. Yiayia smiles and puts it on the wall next to a faded landscape of Crete.

She begins to do some polishing and I ask her if I can help. She hands me a spare duster and we do it together. I dust a stone paperweight which has a picture of some houses on it and some words in Greek that I can't read. One by one, she picks up various framed photographs that sit on her dresser. One of them is me (it is a school photo that I don't like at all), two of them are wedding photos (one of my parents and another of Yiayia and my grandfather, who died when I was small), and there's a very faded one of a family. This last one was at the back and I have never noticed it before. Yiayia sees me staring at it and points out who is who.

"That's me and my sister and our parents," she says. "In Plaka."

I didn't even know she had a sister. My curiosity is aroused. Who is this sister? Does it mean there is a part of the family I have never even met?

"Plaka? Where is that?"

"The place where I grew up," she says. "It's a pretty village, right on the sea."

"In Crete?"

"Yes, agapi mou, very close to here."

"So why don't we ever go there?"

"No special reason," she answers, putting the photos back into their usual places. She seems a bit impatient with her dusting now and drops one of the photos as she puts it back. "I don't think your mum likes it because the beach there doesn't have sand."

It doesn't seem a very good excuse to me.

"Ooh!" she says. "I can smell those biscuits! We don't want them to burn do we?"

She rushes out of the room and into the kitchen.

I don't follow her straightaway. I pick up the oldest of the photos, the one I have not noticed before, and study it more carefully. Yiayia was pretty when she was small and the girl standing next to her was beautiful, with very long hair, like a princess. I wonder what her sister's name is and also what the village where they all lived was like. I put the picture down and go into the kitchen with my mind full of questions.

"Yiayia," I ask boldly. "Can we go to your village?"

I think she might make an excuse, because we have never been before, so I am ready for her to say no.

"I don't see why not," she says, smiling. I am really happy and surprised when she suggests that we go that day. "We can take the bus," she says. "There's one that leaves here early this afternoon."

She seems as eager as me to go on an outing.

The biscuits are almost cool now and we wrap some up to eat on the way and find my swimming costume and a towel in case there is time to paddle. As we get to the bus stop, a greeny-blue bus is coming round the corner. Yiayia pays our fares and we take the front seat to have the best view.

The journey takes us along the coast, so we see lots of sailing boats. Then we go through a village called Elounda, where the bus has to slow down because there are goats in the road. As we are coming into another village, Yiayia struggles to her feet.

"We're here!" she says.

The journey has only taken thirty minutes but we've managed to eat six biscuits each on the way. Yiayia winks at me.

"Don't tell your mum," she laughs.

The bus sets us down right in the middle of Plaka. It isn't very big and the houses are old and some are crumbling. I can see the sea at the end of the little street where we got off the bus and, out in the bay, a small island with buildings on it. Behind us, there are mountains rising up into the sky. We are very thirsty so we sit for a cold drink in a kafeneio (that's Greek for café) under an old pine tree in the square.

The village is small, so from where we are sitting, Yiayia points out places from her childhood including the village school and the houses of her two closest friends.

"My friend Fotini's house used to be a restaurant, they call it a taverna in Greek," she says. "And that's where her mum taught me how to make those biscuits we cooked this morning." Then she points out the paths that lead up the mountains. "We used to go up there to find wildflowers," she says. "The same as the ones you and I still pick sometimes."

"For the tea that mum likes?" I ask.

Yiayia nods.

"And there's the beach. The one your mother doesn't like because it's pebbly," she says with a smile.

Plaka seems a nice, quiet village but I can see why Yiayia moved somewhere with more shops and people.

"The village hasn't changed that much except that it was a lot busier then," says Yiayia. "I have so many memories from growing up here."

And then she begins to tell me about her life. None of it is what I imagine...

OUR HOUSE WAS DOWN THERE RIGHT next to the sea. My father, Giorgos, was a fisherman with his own little boat and my mother, Eleni, was the village schoolteacher. All the children loved her. She was kind and beautiful and a gifted painter. There were several of her pictures of the Cretan countryside on our walls. My sister was five years older than me, and her name was Anna. She was very rebellious and never did what my parents told her. Anna used to tease me for being a "goody-goody" because I did my homework on time and hers was always late. We couldn't have been more different.

Our neighbours were the Andrakis family. There were four children squeezed into a house even smaller than ours and the youngest, Dimitris, was like a brother to me. We were born a few days apart so for my whole life we had been close. He was very shy and always getting teased at school because he was shorter than the other boys and also because he was very clever. When we were doing maths, his hand always shot into the air with a right answer even before the rest of us had written anything down. We played every day and always walked to school together.

I don't have many memories from when I was very small except that when I was six years old, Crete was invaded by the Nazis. It was 1941 and three or four difficult years followed. There was never enough to eat and all of us were thin. My parents were anxious from morning until night and my sister and I often had to hide in a cupboard when Italian or German soldiers came through Plaka.

Many people were killed in nearby villages. Those were dark days, but eventually they came to an end when the enemy left. Once they had gone, it was as if a black cloud had lifted and life was happy once again. I was just ten years old then.

AROUND TWO HUNDRED PEOPLE LIVED in Plaka at that time. There was a bakery, a kafeneio, a taverna and a church, just as now. Once a week, farmers came to the village to sell their vegetables and fruit, and a pedlar came monthly with essential things for the house such as saucepans and brooms. Most families had their own goats so we all had fresh milk and cheese.

On fine days after school, I used to go with Dimitris, my other best friend Fotini, her big brother Pavlos, and his friend Petros up into the mountains behind the village. We picked camomile (for making tea) and sometimes wild horta (like spinach) and, when it rained, snails. I always hated horta but I hated snails even more. So did Anna. When we had snail stew, I used to hide them in my napkin and throw them in a bin when our mother wasn't looking but Anna used to spit them out right in front of our parents.

Summer was heaven. School finished in June so we had very long holidays and day after day we went to the beach, sometimes a whole group of us, and other times just me and Dimitris. We were carefree. Everyone in the village knew everyone else so our parents didn't have any worries about us if we were out for hours at a time. All of us had learned to swim when we were young so we were strong swimmers. We often had races and played our own version of water polo.

Skimming stones was another favourite game and Dimitris and I used to do it for hours and hours every day. He always managed to get twice as many bounces as me, but I could throw a pebble even further than he could.

My father made simple fishing rods for me and Dimitris. Occasionally we even managed to catch a fish or two and proudly took them home to cook.

Whatever games we had been playing, the rule was that we had to be back inside before the sun set.

ONE WARM EVENING, WHEN WE WERE putting on our shoes and socks, Dimitris suddenly pointed out to sea.

"Look, Maria! There's your father!"

I followed the direction in which his finger was pointing. There was nothing unusual in seeing my father's boat bobbing about on the sea, but this time there was something different. I could see the silhouettes of two other people outlined against the darkening sky.

"Who is that with him?" I demanded.

"How should I know?" answered Dimitris. "I am sure your mother will tell you."

Slowly, the boat was approaching the island.

The island's name was Spinalonga and it sat right in the middle of the bay opposite Plaka. Although nobody ever dared, Fotini's brother boasted that if he wanted, he could swim there and back in an hour. And if he swam all the way round, it would take him two. We all knew a few things about the island's past that we learned at school. A very long time ago, the Romans were there, then it became a Venetian castle (and it still had big walls from that time), then some Turks lived there and built houses on it. We were told less about its present.

What the island was used for now was something that the grown-ups did not talk about in front of us, but we all knew that it was a place where very sick people went. It was a hospital for anyone with an incurable disease called leprosy. Dimitris said that on still nights, he had heard screams coming from patients there. I never heard them, but Dimitris never told fibs. As well as a priest, there was only one man who went across and came back. His name was Mr Lidakis. Everyone else was afraid to go because they were scared of catching the disease.

Now, for the first time, I saw my father going there.

When I got home, my mother was cooking. She had a worried look on her face.

"I won at skimming stones!" I said, to try and cheer her up. "And Dimitris nearly caught an octopus."

She didn't seem interested and the frown on her face deepened as she asked me to set the table for three.

"Where's Dad?"

"He won't be back until late. Can you tell Anna supper is ready?"

It was unheard of for my father not to eat with us. Even if he was going to stay out fishing all night, he always ate first.

Eventually, Anna came down from our bedroom, as usual holding a battered fashion magazine. She was always asking Mum for new dresses, and got the same answer each time: "When Dad catches the biggest fish in the ocean, you can have a dozen."

That night, they had an argument about why Anna was reading a magazine rather than her school book and then Mum noticed that Anna had plaited her hair differently.

"If you didn't spend so much time playing with your hair, you would have more time for homework," she said, trying not to sound too cross.

Anna was beautiful and knew it, and was always coming up with new ways to get herself noticed by the boys.

"Do you like it?" Anna asked, spinning round to show us the back. Only then did she notice that our father wasn't there. "Where is Dad?"

"He's taking some sick people to Spinalonga," said Mum.

"Sick people! You mean lepers!" shrieked Anna. "He's taking lepers to the island? Why? Where's Mr Lidakis? That's *his* job!"

Although I knew that Spinalonga was a place for people with leprosy, I didn't know much else. I understood that there was no cure and that only one man, Mr Lidakis, took the patients from Plaka to the island and also went with supplies.

It was more or less banned to talk about leprosy, not only in our family but in all the homes in Plaka. There was so much fear surrounding it. If ever we asked our parents anything, they told us it was a terrible sickness and there was nothing more to be said. I always suspected they knew more than they were telling us. Anna, as usual, broke the rules about not speaking of it.

"He'll catch leprosy!" Anna shrieked. "He'll be cursed! His hands will fall off! He'll go blind! He'll be crippled."

"Stop it, Anna! Mr Lidakis is not well, so your father is doing him a favour."

"Has Mr Lidakis got leprosy? Has he caught it? I bet he has! And now our father will catch it too."

"Anna. Calm down!" Our mother sounded stricter than usual. "Of course he won't catch it," she said.

I was puzzled. We all knew that Mr Lidakis had never caught leprosy but that didn't mean that our father wouldn't. Maybe it was just a matter of luck. And maybe Dad would be unlucky.

We sat down at the table and our mother served us. Anna pushed her food round her plate.

None of us spoke.

WHEN I GOT UP FOR SCHOOL THE next day, Dad was sitting at the table drinking coffee.

He looked just the same as before, still with all his limbs. Even so, I found myself staring at him with curiosity.

"What's the matter, agapi mou?"

"We were worried about you ... you went across to Spinalonga."

"I took two patients. A man and a woman. They'll never leave again so it was very sad."

Why couldn't they leave? How had they caught the disease? What would happen to them?

I asked all these questions: *Why? How? What?* Just as we were encouraged to in science lessons at school. My father answered patiently while my mother sat listening.

"The problem is that there is no treatment and no cure," he explained. "So the government has said that anyone with the disease has to go and live on Spinalonga, in case they pass it to anyone else."

"But what will happen to them?" I insisted.

Science was my favourite subject and I already knew that the only way to understand anything was to keep digging for answers. This was how you got to the bottom of things. I was full of questions about leprosy that day, especially because my father had been across to Spinalonga. For the first time, I was getting proper answers.

"What people are afraid of is partly right," he explained. "Sometimes the disease eats away at your body. In the end you can lose your fingers and toes because you can't feel them any more, so you can't work or even walk."

I couldn't speak. I had assumed my sister was over-reacting as usual. But now I realised she wasn't.

"And that's all I know really," he said. "I left the

couple at the quayside over there and then they went through a tunnel that leads into the rest of the island. I didn't see anything else. Or anyone else."

"Will you go again?" asked my mother quietly.

"No, agapi mou. Mr Lidakis will definitely be better tomorrow."

Anna ran into the room and stopped abruptly in front of our father.

"You're back!" she said, looking him up and down, as if to make sure he was still the same.

"Of course I am, Anna."

She hesitated in front of him. Normally she would have given our father a hug before leaving, but I could see that she still had her suspicions and thought that if he had been with leprosy patients, he might be able to pass on the disease.

"Come on, girls," our mother interrupted. "It's time to leave for school."

MY SISTER AND I ALWAYS WENT TO CHURCH in those days even though we didn't want to. Anna moaned about it every week.

"It goes on all day!" she complained.

"No, it doesn't, Anna," reprimanded my father. "It's only two hours."

"But I want to go to the beach!"

"You can go later," said my mother patiently.

That Sunday, the priest read out a passage from the book of Leviticus in the Old Testament. It said that anyone with leprosy was cursed, that they were unclean and that they should be sent out of the village.

I felt Anna pinching me on the leg.

"You see?" she whispered. "What did I tell you? It's a living death."

I didn't really understand what the Bible was telling us. Did "unclean" just mean "dirty"? Or more than that? And what did Anna mean exactly? How can you be alive and dead at the same time?

It was still a mystery to me. I could not imagine what a leprosy patient even looked like. If they arrived in Plaka from another part of the country and were taken over to the island by Mr Lidakis, they were always covered by a blanket.

I sat on the hard wooden seat in church, listening to the words of the priest. Then my mind began to wander and my imagination to take hold of me. My fear of leprosy and whether Dad might have caught it was greater than before, but I still did not really understand what it was.

GRADUALLY, THESE WORRIES SLIPPED TO
the back of my mind and, soon enough, the summer
holidays began. Anna and some of the other older
children didn't play with us any more and Fotini had to
help her mother a little more in the taverna, so much of
the time it was just me and Dimitris. Several months
stretched ahead of us to play, explore and have fun.

Sometimes my mother packed up some food for us
to take into the mountains. On other days we spent hour
after carefree hour, jumping off the rocks, swimming,
and collecting shells to make necklaces for our mothers.
We were allowed to stay up later that summer and we
often used to lie on the pebbles waiting to see a comet.

One night in July, there was a spectacular show
of falling stars. Every few minutes a bright light flew
across the sky, some leaving a long trail of white. There
were so many that we lost count.

"Look! Look! Maria! Look at that tail!"

"Quick! Quick! Make a wish, Dimitris!"

"You too!" he urged.

I made a wish that my father would be safe when he went out to sea. That was the only thing I ever wanted.

In August there was an eclipse – slowly, slowly the giant, dark red moon was cast into shadow.

"It's like magic!" I said.

"It *is* magic," Dimitris replied.

We were enchanted by everything up above us.

A few days after the eclipse, Anna and I were taken to Elounda for winter shoes, and my mother bought books for the new school year.

And then term began again. Dimitris and I were excited to be learning fresh things. It was the year when we began algebra and geometry, and numbers suddenly came to life. Dimitris turned out to be brilliant at solving equations and my mother started setting him special extra homework.

THE SCHOOL DAY ALWAYS FOLLOWED THE same routine. We started with a song, then my mother said a prayer, then we divided into groups according to age and sat at our desks. One day in October, however, none of these things happened. When we got to school we were all told to form a line. We assumed this was a nit-check. Whenever my mother spotted nits in someone's hair we all had to be inspected. Any boy who was found with them had his head shaved and any girl would be sent home for her mother to go through every strand of hair with a special fine comb. For some weeks, Dimitris had been hiding his head under an old red cap of his brother's. He was still practically bald after a nit-check earlier in the term and had been getting bullied even more than usual.

We soon realised that this was not a hair inspection. That day, a doctor in a white coat and a nurse in a pale blue uniform were waiting for us.

"We need to examine you all today," said the doctor. "There has been an increase in the number of people with leprosy in Greece and the government has instructed that every child must have an examination."

There was some murmuring among the smaller children but from the older ones at the back, including Anna, there were loud protests. The words "catching!" "disease!" "infection!" rang in the air.

"It's nothing to be afraid of, children," said my mother in her gentlest voice. "All the doctor will do is check your skin for any signs. There is only a very small chance you will have it."

In spite of what she said, there were lots of children shouting and some were crying and even though she

was my own mother, I did not believe those words: *"It's nothing to be afraid of."* If there was one thing I knew about leprosy, it was that everyone was terrified of it.

My mother was very cross at the fuss everyone was making and shouted at us all to calm down. This was very unlike her.

One by one she led the children behind a screen. Anna was among the first, being almost the oldest, but she was soon out and smirked at me as she passed, before going out into the school yard.

Dimitris grabbed my hand. He was always shy with strangers.

"Don't worry, Dimitris," I said, squeezing his hand. "You won't be in there for long."

After half an hour or so, it was my turn. I had to stand in my underwear while the doctor examined my legs and arms and torso. He used something like a magnifying glass and soon he was done. My mother smiled as she saw the doctor put a line through my name.

I got dressed again and loitered in the schoolroom. Almost everyone was out in the yard now, and I could see them running about in the morning sunshine. Only a few were left to be checked. Dimitris was among them. I waited while he went behind the screen. And waited. And waited. The others who were still in the queue were getting restless and had begun to play chase around the room, weaving in and out of the desks and sending chairs flying.

MY MOTHER CAME OUT FROM BEHIND
the screen. She was very pale and at first I thought
it was anger at seeing the commotion her pupils
were creating. She clapped her hands sharply to make the
remaining children form a line again.

I saw Dimitris come out and immediately dash
through the door. I chased after him and soon found
him in the corner of the school yard, his face hidden
beneath his cap. He was crying.

I sat next to him on a low wall, put my arm round
him and felt the sobs that rocked his body.

"Dimitris ... Dimitris ... it's all right. It's all done
now."

He wouldn't speak.

The examinations must have been completed because my mother appeared and hurried towards us.

"Maria, please get up and go and play with your other friends," she said sternly. "I need to take Dimitris home. If they ask, tell the children that I will be back very shortly and lessons will start then."

I had no wish to play and stayed alone in the corner of the school yard, from where I could see the gate and keep an eye for her return. It was impossible not to think about Dimitris. Did my best friend, the boy who was like a brother to me, have leprosy? I was struggling to believe this. Surely there had to be some mistake?

When she returned, my mother took us all inside to finish the day's lessons, but as soon as the bell rang for the end of the school day, I raced up to her.

"I will tell you what's happened, Maria. But only

when everyone else has gone," she said. I had never seen this look on my mother's face. It was a mixture of sadness and fear.

Anna had already left and soon enough the school was silent. My mother gathered up some exercise books for marking and turned out the light. Taking my hand, together we began the short walk to our house.

When we were halfway there we stopped, went down to the beach and sat on the pebbles.

"I'm so sorry, Maria," she murmured. "Dimitris has leprosy. In a few days he will go to Spinalonga."

I felt sick. This could not be happening. It couldn't be true!

For a moment I couldn't speak. There was nothing I could think of to say. I didn't even cry because I was so shocked.

"I know how much you'll miss him," she said. It was only then that I realised my mother was weeping.

I stared at my shoes as we walked home and then noticed that they were covered in splashes. It took a moment to realise that these were my tears. I was crying too. In my whole life, nothing so terrible had happened. My best friend had caught the incurable disease and soon he would leave for ever.

At dinner that evening, everyone was too sad to speak and none of us had any appetite, even Anna who always ate more than anyone. Dad went out on his boat that night. There was no moon so it would be a good time to fish.

The doctor had given my mother a leaflet about leprosy, which now lay on the kitchen table. Finally, my curiosity could be satisfied. On the first page it showed some photographs of how the disease might look at the beginning. In one of them it showed a child's leg. It looked completely normal except for an area of skin which was paler than the rest. Was that really all it was?

Was this all that Dimitris had? As I flicked through the rest of the leaflet, I saw images of more extreme cases. Some of the people shown were badly disfigured.

There was information about using sulphur to disinfect anything that had been touched by someone with leprosy, but the leaflet kept on repeating that anyone diagnosed must be isolated. Isolation was the only solution. There was no cure.

I put the leaflet down. I wished I had not read it at all.

Eventually, I got up and put my arm around my mother to say goodnight.

"Goodnight, agapi mou. Try not to worry about Dimitris. He will be looked after well on Spinalonga."

She stood up to hug me and I began to cry for the second time that day.

"Agapi mou! My darling! I know it's sad but we must try to be brave for Dimitris."

My tears kept flowing and my mother held me tighter and tighter. After a while, I went up to bed but I could not sleep. My heart was full of sadness and my pillow was wet with tears.

Very late in the evening, I heard the bang of the door then my mother's raised voice. She was scolding Anna for coming in late again. After that I fell asleep and then had a nightmare about being in a strange place. I was playing hide and seek with Dimitris, but he was nowhere to be found.

Anna and I slept in the same room and she leant across to poke me.

"Shhh!" she said. "Stop shouting! I want my beauty sleep!"

THE FOLLOWING DAY WAS A HOLIDAY SO there was no school. When I got up, my mother was sitting at the kitchen table marking books as usual, and it was only then that I noticed something strange. Below the place where her hair was swept up, there was a mark! A pale mark, just like the one in the photo. Perhaps it was nothing. Or was it leprosy? What should I do? She was busy marking sums but glanced up at me.

I felt tongue-tied but eventually managed to speak.

"Mum, there is something on your neck. A mark."

She hurried across the room to the mirror.

"It's round the back," I said.

She craned her neck to try and see.

"I can't feel anything," she said, optimistically.

"But isn't that what the leaflet says? That the patch goes numb?"

Just at that moment, Anna burst into the room.

"What are you doing, Mum?"

"Nothing, agapi mou. Just tidying my hair."

"I'm going out," said Anna.

"Going out?"

"For a walk. With Antonis."

"Alright. But be back before dark, not like yesterday."

Antonis was the baker's son and now worked in the family shop. Anna had started going for strolls with him and even for rides on his motorcycle (though my parents didn't know that). Our father did not like him at all and made it clear that he thought Anna was too young to have a boyfriend. As usual, she didn't care what anybody thought, especially our parents.

"Look, Maria," said my mother, as soon as Anna had slammed the door behind her, "I will go and see the doctor tomorrow and ask him to take a look, but will you promise me to keep this a secret until then? I am sure it's nothing."

"Yes..." I said. "I promise."

I HAD ANOTHER ALMOST SLEEPLESS NIGHT AND when I woke up the next day, Mum had already left for the doctor.

I wanted desperately to say goodbye to Dimitris but when I went next door, all the shutters on his house were tightly closed. I knocked. Eventually, the door was opened just a small crack and I could see two dark eyes. It was one of Dimitris's brothers.

"Go away," he said.

"But..." I protested, as the door was shut in my face.

Strolling down to the beach, I aimlessly threw some stones into the sea. How could life have changed so suddenly? I looked across at Spinalonga. It was impossible to imagine that it was to be my best friend's new home, a place so near and yet so far, but I couldn't let myself cry again. There was time to kill while I waited for my mother to return. I picked up a big, flat pebble from the beach and suddenly had an idea.

Back in the house, I got out my paints and began to mix some colours. It was very silent and I concentrated hard to create the image I wanted. The stone had a very smooth surface and soon, with the help of a fine brush, I made a pretty picture.

Several hours later, when daylight was fading a little, I rested my brush in the mug of water. I had done a picture of our house and of Dimitris's house too and beneath it I had painted the words: *Every day I will think of you.* I left it to dry on the shelf by the window and went outside to wait for the bus that would bring my mother back from the doctor.

I didn't have to wait long. Soon the familiar greeny-blue bus was coming down the road. It stopped by the church and I saw my mother get off. My legs were shaking as she approached. Before she said anything, I knew the truth. It was written on her face and even in the way she walked towards me, her head bent.

I realised that she could not hug me and that she would never hug me again, but I was determined to be brave. It wasn't easy and we walked the short distance to our house in silence. Even when we got there, we didn't say a word.

My mother stood at the stove and began to stir a pot of fish stew and I watched as she stirred and stirred and stirred some more, her mind very far away.

Suddenly I heard the latch being lifted. It was my father. I was sitting in the corner pretending to read and heard my mother breaking the news to him. In that instant, his face and his hair seemed to turn grey. For a while they talked in voices so low that I couldn't hear them. I think Dad's heart broke that day.

When Anna eventually arrived back and was told that Mum had leprosy she started screaming and crying. Our father sent her upstairs. It was a terrible day, but the next one was worse.

Our mother packed only a few things. I saw her carefully wrap one of four china cups with a rose pattern which we used on special occasions and I knew what she was thinking: that if she drank from it there on the island and we used the others here, we would all somehow be together.

Then I remembered the pebble I had painted. Instead of giving it to Dimitris as I had planned, I handed it to her.

I watched her eyes flicker over the words:

Every day I will think of you.

"Promise me you will," she said.

I saw that she was trying to smile, but she couldn't manage. She ended up looking even sadder than if she hadn't tried at all.

I remembered occasions in the past when I had been crying and my mother had told me to be brave. I could see now that she was finding it as hard as me not to weep.

"Yes, I promise." I said it with as much courage as I could. I felt I needed to be strong for her.

"And my promise is that I will write to you often," she said.

On Monday morning, she left the house without kissing us goodbye because she was afraid we would catch leprosy. She was wearing her favourite blue shawl. It was made of soft, light wool from a special type of goat and whenever she wore it I loved to feel it against my face. It was very precious to her because Dad had given it to her a long time ago.

Dimitris was waiting in the street outside with his parents and I saw my mother take his hand. His parents then went back inside their house and shut the door. It gave me a funny feeling, seeing my mother holding my best friend's hand and knowing that she would never again hold mine. I wanted to run after them. Dimitris looked very small next to her, his red cap pulled down over his eyes, and I wanted to shout their names to make them both look round. But I didn't, and they kept walking.

My father told me and Anna to go back inside the house. My mother had told us very firmly that she did not want us to come to the quayside, so from our window the three of us watched Mr Lidakis's boat making its way across the sea to the island.

We stayed there gazing out of the window for a long time and, when we saw the boat on its way back, we knew that Mum and Dimitris were now inside the walls of Spinalonga.

THE FOLLOWING DAY, WHEN I LEFT THE house for school, I waved from our front steps in the direction of the island. I did the same thing each day, but I couldn't see if anyone returned the wave.

After a few weeks Mr Lidakis brought us an envelope. It had come from Spinalonga and had a really strange smell, just like a stink bomb.

"It's been disinfected," he said to our father. It was what they did with letters from the island to get rid of the bacteria.

Anna was out so I carefully slit open the envelope. It was from our mother.

My darling girls,
I hope you are all managing
How is the new schoolteacher? Maria,
have you learned some new equations?
Anna, did you write your essay?
Life here is very different. I have
been given a small house, and I live
here with Dimitris. I am keeping up with
his lessons. Yesterday was his saint's day
and someone made a cake. There is a baker
here and supplies are brought over by
Mr. Lidakis so there is enough to eat.
I will write again
very soon.
With love,
Mum

I felt a pang of jealousy at the thought of Dimitris getting all of our mother's attention and then I felt ashamed. I was still reading the letter when Anna came in. Impatient to see it, she snatched it out of my hand and it ripped in half.

Our father, who was trying to prepare something to eat, shouted at us both and Anna ran out of the house crying. I felt guilty that I had opened the envelope before she arrived. It didn't take much to provoke a tantrum with Anna.

I wrote back to our mother that afternoon. I tried to sound cheerful, but it was difficult. I told her that Dimitris's mother was often cooking for us now and that the new schoolteacher was good, but not as good as her.

I didn't tell her that some of the children ran away every time either Anna or I were anywhere near them. I had heard the word "stigma" used by grown-ups but now I really knew what it meant. If you had a relative with leprosy, people shunned you. Anyway, I mentioned none of that. The most important thing was to tell her that I always waved as I left home to go to school.

When the next envelope came, there were two letters inside: one for me and one for Anna.

Dear Maria,

I was so happy to see you yesterday! I saw you waving and I will come and wave too – every day at exactly eight o clock. And afterwards, I will go back to the house and drink from my little rose cup. Next week I will start to teach some of the children here, and Dimitris will begin lessons again.

Love
Mum

P.S. We found a kitten up on the hill. He was all alone so he has come to live with us.

The next day at the usual time, I was on the steps waving frantically. At first I couldn't see anyone on the other side but, as I peered into the distance, I could suddenly make something out. It was like a blue flag. I realised it was my mother. She was waving her shawl – the one I knew she had taken with her! I was so happy. I waved and waved until I thought my arm was going to drop off! And then my father appeared at the door.

"Maria! What are you doing? You'll be late for school!"

"Look!" I said. "It's Mum! Remember her blue shawl?"

"Yes," Dad said as he looked across towards Spinalonga. "You're right. It's her!"

For just a moment, I saw a smile on his face. It was the first time since Mum had left. Anna then came out and all three of us waved across towards the island.

"You must both go now," said our father after a little while. "I am sure she will be back another day."

"She'll be there tomorrow," I said firmly. "She made a promise!"

Each day after that, we saw the flash of blue. And each day it lifted our spirits.

I WROTE TO MY MOTHER EVERY WEEK and told her everything I was doing, and she did the same. She often sent me sums to solve and in my reply I gave her my answers. Sometimes I sent her a piece of embroidery, even though my stitches were clumsy.

Mum was a good artist and one day a letter arrived with pictures showing how Spinalonga looked. I was amazed. It had a street just like ours in Plaka and a kafeneio and a church. In the next letter she sent a painting of her own house, with geraniums in a pot outside, and in the one after that she did a drawing of a kitten who spent most of the day asleep on her doorstep. In another, she drew the island governor's house with its grand balcony. After many months, I felt that I knew every nook and cranny of Spinalonga. It looked very like our own village but with even more flowers!

Dimitris and I began to write to each other too. I told him news of school, what the teacher who had come to replace my mother was like, what some of our friends were doing. And he told me things about Spinalonga, who his new friends were (he was not the only child there) and what they did at school. He told

me that they had named the kitten "Asteri", Star. One summer night, there was a shooting star and we both wrote about it in our letters. We agreed that it was even bigger and brighter than any we had seen the previous summer. He had made a chart of when the moon was going to be full in the next few months and sent me the dates. Every time it happened, we would be looking at it together.

I asked him to come and wave when my mother did. Sometimes they looked very far away, but on clear days it was easy to make Dimitris out, the red dot of his cap telling me that it was him. It was like a distant planet in the night sky.

SEVERAL YEARS PASSED LIKE THIS. IT WAS a strange life but we had to accept the situation. I worked hard at my lessons and read in the evenings. I also tried to keep the house tidy and sometimes cooked something if my father was on an all-night fishing trip. Anna was out most of the time with her boyfriend and my father was cross with her but there seemed little he could do.

The best moment of the week was when a letter arrived from Mum. The drawings that came with them were beautiful and I stuck them all in a scrapbook.

Dimitris's letters were precious too and I kept them in a box. The years were passing by, but our friendship remained just as close. We were like a brother and sister but without the arguing! We shared all our hopes and dreams.

Sometimes there were people in my mother's drawings and I studied them carefully. What did they look like? Had they lost arms and legs and fingers and toes? Most of the women had scarves over their heads so it was hard to see their faces and some of the elderly men had walking sticks. They could have been the old people of Plaka. They looked similar.

One day, she sent a portrait of Dimitris. In some ways he had changed a lot. His hair had grown and now he wore glasses. In other ways he looked just the same.

Leprosy. I was curious. If it hadn't altered him, why couldn't he come back? Did my mother still look the same? If she did, then why couldn't she come back too?

When I asked Dad this, he told me that there were still no drugs to cure the disease. Once they had been diagnosed with leprosy, a patient could not return, even if they showed no obvious signs of sickness. I thought this was very unfair and told him so.

The next big change in our family was that, as soon as she was eighteen, Anna got married to Antonis and moved out. Now I had a room all to myself and it was a little more peaceful in the house. Even though we had been fighting since we were little, I missed my sister being there. And I think my father did too.

A few months later, I was tidying up the things Anna had left behind and I found the pictures that Mum had sent to Anna stuffed in a drawer. I knew then how ashamed she was that Mum was on Spinalonga.

A YEAR OR SO AFTER, I NOTICED A CHANGE in my mother's drawings. They became less detailed. They even began to remind me of the sketches that I had done when I was small. It was strange. I wanted to ask her why, but part of me didn't want to know the answer. Even her handwriting had begun to alter.

A while later, Dimitris began to write her letters for her.

Dear Maria
I haven't done a drawing for this week.
I hope you dont mid.
At the moment I am finding it hard to hold a pencil. I hope this will get better soon.
Dimitris brings me camomile tea in my rose jug, every day.
Love Mum

Each morning we still waved. At eight o'clock, when I left the house, there it was across the water: the familiar blue shawl and a dot of red. Dimitris must have grown into that cap by now.

Then, one day that winter, neither of them appeared. Perhaps they had forgotten. Perhaps they thought the weather was too bad. I came up with all sorts of reasons. But when they did not come for five days in a row, I knew something bad had happened.

A letter arrived and inside the envelope there was a single sheet. Usually there were three, one each for my father, Anna and me. It was Dimitris's handwriting on the envelope, as usual, and I watched Dad reading, anxiously waiting for him to share my mother's news.

Suddenly his body seemed to crumple, just like the paper he now held to his chest.

Eventually, I took the letter from his hands and read it for myself. Dimitris explained that, in recent weeks, my mother's leprosy had changed from the mild to the severe type. The disease had taken her away very rapidly, he said, and there had been nothing anyone could do. I read and then re-read the letter. I was totally numb with disbelief.

Even though she was across the sea for all those years, it was very hard to accept that my mother had actually gone. I would never

again see her waving the bright blue shawl or imagine her sipping tea from her rose cup. I thought of Dimitris too. Would he miss her even more than us? She had cared for him and been a mother to him as well as his teacher for so many years. At least my father and I still had each other. Dimitris was now alone.

That afternoon, I went up into the mountains and gathered an armful of wildflowers. Using a piece of dried grass to tie them, I made a beautiful bouquet and went down to the beach. I stood for a while looking out at Spinalonga and then threw the flowers as far as I could into the sea. For a while they were tossed on the waves. Up and down they went, side to side, and little by little they floated further and further towards the island. I stood and watched them until finally they disappeared from sight.

ANNA WAS SEVEN MONTHS PREGNANT
when Mum died. When she was told the news, all she
said was that she did not want her child ever to know
that her grandmother had died of leprosy. The stigma
was all she seemed to care about.

Life for my father and me did not change. I came
home from school each day to make our supper and
then sat down and did my homework. I was fifteen now
and had decided that I would study hardest at science
because I had set my heart on becoming a doctor. More
than anything I wanted to find a cure for leprosy, so that
patients and their families no longer suffered as we had.
That was my goal.

Dimitris wrote more often now, sharing news of the
island and what was happening there. Spinalonga now
had a generator for electricity, a library and even its own
newspaper. He didn't send drawings like my mother but
I treasured his letters.

He told me that he had received a letter from his parents who had asked him to stop writing. They no longer wished to communicate with him as the stigma was too great. I was shocked that anyone could reject their own child and avoided Dimitris's parents after that. I knew that they were not the only people in the village who wanted nothing to do with leprosy. There were several who crossed the road to avoid me, simply because my mother had died of the disease.

Even though Anna detested her connection with leprosy, she did come round every Sunday with her child. When she came, I always put out the best cups, the ones with the roses that matched the one our mother had taken across to Spinalonga.

One Sunday, she was there as usual. The baby was nine months old and starting to crawl.

Anna was bending down to pick her up off the floor and suddenly she shrieked.

"Maria! Look at your leg!"

She snatched her child into her arms.

"You know what that looks like?" she said, pointing. "I won't say the word in front of my daughter. But you know *exactly* what it is!"

Without saying goodbye, she immediately left the house. My father and I were shocked both by her rudeness, and also by what she had noticed.

We both took a look at the back of my leg to see what Anna was referring to. And there it was: a mark about the size and shape of a strawberry. I touched it. It was totally numb. No wonder I hadn't spotted it before.

The following day, I took the bus to Elounda with my father. I was trembling as I sat in the doctor's waiting room and when the diagnosis came it was what we feared. It had happened to me, just as it had for my mother and Dimitris before me. It was leprosy.

Neither of us spoke on the journey home and the

house remained silent as I packed a few things for the journey to Spinalonga. I'm not sure that either of us could believe what was happening. I took as many science books as I could pack into my bag and my father promised that he would send over some more when I needed them. I did not go round the village to say goodbye to my friends. They would not be able to embrace me. And I did not want to see the look of fear on their faces when they saw me. I wanted to remember them as they were and the other way round too. I would write letters when I got there.

"We will both be strong," I said to my father, putting on a brave face.

In spite of our courageous words, Dad and I shed a sea of tears that night. He promised that he would come and wave to me each morning, just as we had waved to my mother. At dawn the next day, he took me over to the island.

EVEN BEFORE THE BOAT WAS TETHERED, I could see Dimitris waiting for me at the entrance to Spinalonga. More than half a decade had passed since we had seen each other but we hugged just as we had done as children. We were overjoyed. All through those years, our letters had kept us very close. We knew all about each other's lives from writing to each other and I realised immediately that our friendship had not changed. He was still my best friend.

He took me through the long dark tunnel which led into the island. I had seen it from a distance for my whole life and it seemed strange to be so close now. When we emerged into the light, I felt as though I was somewhere I knew as well as my own village. I saw for myself everything that my mother had shown me in her drawings: the pretty houses with their brightly painted shutters and doors, the flowering geraniums in big pots, the little shops, the bakery with its rows of loaves, the kafeneio, the church of Saint Panteleimon, the patron saint of healing. It was even more beautiful than Plaka!

There were a few children skipping down the street, and many older people sitting in their doorways. Dimitris stopped to introduce me to them. They smiled and one of them held out her hand. I saw that her fingers were very bent and tried not to stare. Another woman came up to say hello, but she did not lift the veil that covered her face and greeted us leaning on her crutches. I noticed that she had lost a foot.

"You are going to come and live in the same house where I lived with your mother," said Dimitris. "There are two bedrooms and plenty of space."

Dimitris was so cheerful that I could only smile too. He was sad, of course, that I had the disease, but happy that we were reunited.

When we got to the house, I saw something that was familiar from my mother's drawings. It was Asteri, a fully grown cat now, and she was waiting on the doorstep for us.

It was strange to see my mother's things still set out in the living room. The house was well kept, with flowery curtains and a cloth on the table that I remembered from home. There were framed photographs of me and Anna, and one of our parents on their wedding day. On the shelf I noticed the rose cup sitting next to the pebble which I had painted all those years before. I arranged my books next to them. It was very comforting to see these familiar objects and this made the house feel more like home. On that first evening, Asteri curled up on my lap and purred, as if she knew me.

IN THE FIRST FEW DAYS, I LEARNED MORE about Spinalonga. I met the governor of the island, and the man who wrote the weekly newspaper. People had been sent here from all over Greece, and many had accents I had never heard before, coming from Athens or faraway islands like Naxos. They had done all sorts of jobs. There was an engineer, a poet, even an actor.

Dimitris showed me the school where he was now the teacher. It looked exactly like our school in Plaka. Then I went to visit the hospital which was a big building high up on the hill. My mother had never sent us a drawing of it.

Several women who were still fit and able were helping with patients who had become too sick to be at home. I spoke to one of the nurses and said that I would be very happy to help out. The next day, I was instructed on how to clean and dress the sores that so many people suffered from, and after that I began to go every day.

At eight o'clock in the morning, I left the house, stopped to wave to my father and then climbed the hill to the hospital. In the evening, when I returned home, Dimitris would cook supper because he was home first and very good at making the most of very little. We had meat once a week, and fish twice (I always shared mine with Asteri). Dimitris was a better cook than me, so I was happy for him to play the role of chef, and over our meal he would entertain me with funny stories about his school. The children here were no different from those on the mainland and got up to all the same tricks and truancies.

My stories from the hospital were more serious. From time to time we "lost" one of the nurses because they became sick, and sometimes the days were very long. But I was young and had plenty of energy. Without a cure, all we could do was keep the sores that patients developed clean and try not to let them become infected.

The years went by and I started teaching other people how to nurse the sick and began making detailed notes on patients' symptoms and treatment.

I read as much as I could about leprosy. Thousands of people in many countries around the world suffered from it and doctors everywhere were trying to find a cure.

My father did all he could to find me medical books and journals and he gave them to Mr Lidakis to bring across, along with supplies for the island.

I used to look forward to receiving these packages. In one journal, an article announced that a medicine that cured our illness had been found in America. A few months later, there was another article. It was not such good news. It said that when this same medicine was tried on patients in a hospital like ours, many of them became even sicker. As sometimes happens with drugs, there are times when they do not work as well as first hoped. The cure had not been found after all.

ONE SUNNY SPRING MORNING, WHEN THE SEA was calm and the hillside on Spinalonga was covered with bright yellow flowers, I stood to wave to my father. In the distance I could see him waving back. I noticed that Mr Lidakis was coming over not just with supplies but with a new patient too. It made me sad whenever someone came to begin their life of exile on the island.

I continued on my way to the hospital and was very busy bandaging a woman's foot, when one of the other helpers ran into the room.

"There's a doctor! A doctor has come!" she cried out with excitement.

We had not had a doctor on Spinalonga before because there was nothing to treat us with, so I was very surprised. Most people were too afraid to come near us.

As we were talking, a young man I had never seen before strode into the ward.

He was very smart, with a dark suit and a brimmed hat. When he lifted it to greet me, I noticed his deep brown eyes and handsome face.

He held out his hand to shake mine. I was astonished. Why would anyone who was well want to touch me?

"I am Doctor Kyritsis. Very nice to meet you," he said.

"I am Maria. And this is Kyria Vasso," I said, indicating the patient I was helping.

He watched me as I finished bandaging the woman's foot and, once I had done so, asked me to show him around the hospital. For some reason I found myself shaking. I don't know why, but he made me feel nervous even though he was obviously a kind person.

"I am going to live here," he said. "I want to study the patients and find out about each one of them and about how their leprosy progresses. It is important for my research. Do you keep records?"

I told him that I had started making notes on some of the patients in the hospital. For the first time Doctor Kyritsis smiled. We spent the day going through the files and then began to organise a room that would be his office. In the evening, we went to see the governor, who found an empty house for him.

Soon after that, I became his assistant.

One day, I told Doctor Kyritsis all about my own mother and how I dreamed of finding a cure for this disease.

"We both have the same aim then," he said. "Let's do this together."

As he said this, he took my hand. My heart was racing. I was very excited that finally there was hope. Perhaps one day I might be able to go home.

OVER THE NEXT FEW MONTHS, I SPENT most of my waking hours with the doctor and I learned something new from him every day. He showed me how to treat sores more effectively and how to help people when they found it hard to breathe. We could not stop people dying, but at least we could relieve their discomfort.

Doctor Kyritsis shook hands with everyone without fear or stigma. The patients liked him and we all agreed what a wonderful person he was. Apart from anything, he risked his own life being here with us.

I woke up each morning looking forward to my day in the hospital. Although there was still no cure, my life had purpose now and I was happy and excited to be

working with this kind and clever man who gave us all hope and stopped us feeling abandoned. Even Dimitris commented that I seemed to smile more.

But one morning, when I looked across the water to wave to my father as usual, my heart sank. I saw that Doctor Kyritsis was on the boat with Mr Lidakis. The man who had come to help us had left the island!

I stood there watching, feeling as if all hope had gone. I went to the hospital and carried on as normal, but everyone asked me why I looked so sad. I could not tell them the reason, because then they would be sad too.

Dimitris tried to cheer me up that evening by making my favourite spinach pie, but nothing helped. I felt that the world had come to an end.

Some months went by. There was no news from the doctor and everyone was asking me when he might return. I could not tell them because I did not know myself.

Many people had got sicker and the hospital was full. My father was still sending me any information he could and one day he found a small article in a newspaper. Far away, almost on the other side of the world, there had been a meeting of all the leprosy doctors and scientists. It seemed they had made a discovery.

My hands shook when I read this. I did not share the news with the patients but I wondered if that was where Doctor Kyritsis had gone. It was my only hope.

A few weeks later, I went to the hospital to begin my day's work. And there was Doctor Kyritsis, already in the office, as though he had never been away. My heart missed a beat.

"You're back!" I said, unable to suppress my joy.

He looked up and smiled.

"Yes," he said. "And we have lots of work to do."

We walked together through the wards, and he greeted each patient to find out how they were feeling and to examine any wounds. I was very pleased to help him, and when he had finished we went back to the office to make a list of the patients whom he wanted to take part in an "experiment".

"They have to be showing signs of the disease," he said. "But not be too sick."

There was a new drug but it had not been tried on many people.

"The danger," he said, "is that we don't know about the side effects. There is a chance that it could make some patients worse."

"I want to be part of the test," I said. "Especially now that the mark on my leg has started to spread."

The doctor examined my leg and I could see how anxious he was.

"You're right," he said. "But I don't want you to take part." I could not argue. But I was puzzled.

Dimitris wanted to volunteer too but I persuaded him to wait. There were twenty children in the school now and they all depended on him. After a few days, the patients Doctor Kyritsis had selected for the test had all agreed to be guinea pigs. Everyone on Spinalonga knew that this was our only hope. All the ones chosen knew there was a risk, but they were willing to take it. They did it for the rest of us.

TEN PATIENTS BEGAN TO TAKE THE PILLS and each day we watched carefully to see if they had any effect. For several weeks, there seemed to be no change. Then some of them began to get painful red sores and fever and refused to continue with the drugs.

I could see that Doctor Kyritsis was anxious. It was the first time I had seen him look even a little bit worried and I didn't like to see him this way. Now it was me who was trying to reassure him, not the other way round.

"You said it might not work immediately," I said.

"I think I need a new group of patients for the next trial," he said, sounding despondent. "But the only way forward is with an even stronger dose."

All the patients refused because they thought it was making the others ill.

"Let me try it!" I pleaded with the doctor. "I don't mind trying a stronger dose!"

I wanted to help him very badly.

"If there is no cure, then none of us will ever leave. So what do I lose?" I said.

"It's a risk, Maria," he said. "But if it works, then the whole of Spinalonga will owe their lives to you."

He began the treatment immediately. On the first day, I lay there and wondered what it would be like if I was cured. It would mean leaving Spinalonga. I would be happy to go back to Plaka, to see my father and return to normal life. It would also mean, however, that I would never see the doctor again and this made me feel very sad.

That afternoon, when the school day finished, Dimitris came up to the hospital to see me. He brought me fresh clothes and some of my favourite books.

"Maria! You're so pale!" he exclaimed, with real concern in his voice. I had not seen a mirror but he told me afterwards that I looked as white as snow.

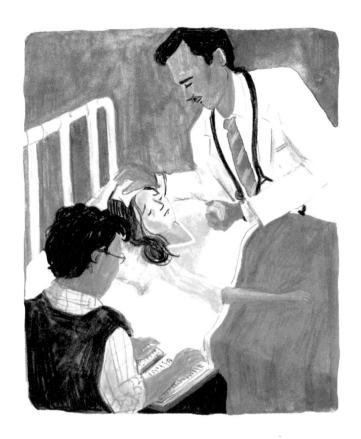

I had begun to feel sick very soon after taking the first dose and for several days I lay in my hospital bed with a high temperature wondering if I would die. The mark on my leg began to grow.

Doctor Kyritsis came to see me each morning and night and very gently mopped my brow with a cold cloth. It made me feel better for a short while, but soon I felt just as before.

TWO WEEKS WENT BY AND THERE WAS NO
improvement in my condition. My temperature never
dropped and Doctor Kyritsis began to look worried.

"Should I stop taking the drugs?" I asked. My voice
was weak.

The doctor shook his head slowly.

"Let's try to carry on a little longer," he said.

A few days later, when Doctor Kyritsis took my
temperature, it was a little lower. He then asked if he
could examine my leg.

I lifted the sheet so that he could see the mark.

"Sorry," he said. "This is the wrong leg. I need to
see the one with the sores."

"But this *is* my infected leg," I said, craning my
neck to try and see the back of my calf. I put my hand
out to feel it too, even though I didn't usually like to do
so. It was always strange to touch a part of you that was
numb.

I saw a strange expression on his face: a mixture of joy and disbelief.

It was a few moments before he could speak.

"It's gone. The patch has disappeared."

"Disappeared?" I echoed. "It can't have disappeared."

"Well, there is nothing on your leg. Not even a small mark." Doctor Kyritsis held my hand and I could feel him trembling. "Maria, I think the drugs have worked." He was obviously happy but I could see that there were tears in his eyes.

"You mean I am ... cured?"

He nodded.

I could not take this in. It had seemed impossible until this moment.

"We must tell everyone!" I said, eagerly.

I was happy for myself but what I really wanted was to get everyone else started on the drugs so that they would all be cured too.

"It might not work for everyone, so I would prefer not to tell them yet," muttered Doctor Kyritsis quietly. "I need to take back this result to the other doctors and then decide what the best dose will be for each patient."

"But can I leave the hospital today?"

"Yes, but I want you to come back as soon as we begin with the others. I will need you."

The way he asked was strange. There was a note of desperation in his voice as if he expected me to disappear. Nothing was further from my mind.

"I will stay on Spinalonga as long as you want me to," I said. There was nothing in my mind other than staying here to be with him. I knew he needed my help, and I wanted to be by his side.

"Thank you, Maria. You took a very big risk to do the test. The next stage is for everyone to be put on the drugs. This is just the beginning!"

DOCTOR KYRITSIS WAS AWAY FOR MANY
weeks and I couldn't wait for his return. Time seemed
to go slower than in all my years on Spinalonga. The
hospital had a very good view of Plaka and I looked
out for him every day from the window, praying that

108

I might see him in Mr Lidakis's little boat. I was impatient to have him back again.

Eventually, my hope was fulfilled. I was on my way up the hill to the hospital one day when I heard a familiar voice behind me.

"Maria!"

I spun around. To my delight it was Doctor Kyritsis and I had to prevent myself from hugging him.

He seemed happy to see me too and told me that, down by the quay, there were two crates. It was a supply of drugs big enough for all the patients on the island. That afternoon, we began the challenging task of starting everyone on the treatment.

Some people were cured very quickly and others, as he had predicted, had a bad reaction to the medicine. It was not an easy time, even though there was so much hope surrounding these drugs. Dimitris was one of those who had a negative reaction and I helped nurse him through many difficult days. Some of the older people, or those with more advanced leprosy, even died which made the rest of us very sad.

After a few months, though, everyone had been treated and most were cured. Of course, I was very glad but I did wish my mother had lived long enough to benefit from the treatment.

We began to talk about leaving Spinalonga. It will sound strange but many of us realised how much we had grown to love our island and each other, and we knew that it was going to be sad saying goodbye. Also, we were aware that in this place we all had something in common: the disease. In the outside world, this would mark us out as different and we knew there would be new difficulties and stigma to face.

For now, though, we had to celebrate that we were cured. This, after all, was a miracle.

I had a letter from my father telling me how excited he was that I was returning. But he also warned that there was an atmosphere of fear in Plaka. People were still afraid of leprosy even though there was now a cure.

Dimitris had written to the teacher in Plaka to ask if he could come and work there, but she had refused to let him anywhere near the school. The disease had been cured but the stigma remained.

One morning in early autumn, we all gathered by the quayside in Spinalonga. Many patients needed help with walking and several were in wheelchairs, but everyone managed to get there. There were many tearful goodbyes as people prepared to leave.

We had been a close community and now we would be scattered far and wide around Greece.

Along with Mr Lidakis, my father would be ferrying people across, eight at a time. With several hundred of us, it would take a few hours.

WHEN MY FATHER ARRIVED, HE TETHERED his boat and came ashore. We embraced and, for a few minutes, we couldn't let go of each other. It was nearly ten years since we had spoken face to face and both of us were overjoyed. He seemed a lot older, with more lines on his face and his hair was now totally white.

"It's time to go," he said, taking my hand. There were queues waiting to get in the boats but he wanted me to be the first.

Suddenly I did not feel ready to leave. Why was my heart heavy when it should have been light? My dream had come true, hadn't it?

"I'll wait until last, Dad," I said. "There is something I have to do." I turned and walked away from the crowds of people.

Sitting at a small table under a tree close by was Doctor Kyritsis. He was handing each patient a signed certificate of clean health.

He looked up and smiled when he realised I was standing there.

"Thank you, Doctor Kyritsis," I said. "For everything."

"Maria," he said. "Without you, this wouldn't be happening. And you are not my patient any longer. Please, call me Nikos."

"We made a good team," I said, turning away. I didn't want him to see my tears.

Years before, I had cried leaving Plaka and saying goodbye to my father. Now, I was crying at the thought of leaving Spinalonga and saying goodbye to Doctor Kyritsis, or Nikos as he had asked me to call him.

I admitted to myself that I was longing to leave Spinalonga, but the idea of not seeing this kind and brilliant man again made me want to weep. He had saved my life and I knew I would miss him.

EVENTUALLY, ALL THE OTHER PATIENTS had been ferried over to Plaka and I was the only one remaining, along with Asteri who trotted next to me, determined not to be left behind. There were just two people left on the whole island: me and Nikos. It was a strange thought that this place where hundreds of people had been living until now was totally empty, except for us. The shops, the church and the kafeneio were all closed up now.

I began walking back towards the quayside to wait for my father to return. I looked down into the water at my feet, turquoise and sparkling, and wondered what the future held.

I heard footsteps and turned around to see Nikos. He looked nervous. I had never seen him so unsure of himself.

"Maria. I can't say goodbye to you."

I didn't know what to say. Was he saying what I hoped he was saying?

It was then that I knew why I had been feeling so sad about leaving Spinalonga. I too had not wanted to say goodbye.

"Will you marry me?" he asked.

I had no doubts about wanting to be with the doctor.

"Yes," I said, without hesitation.

It is impossible to describe how joyful and optimistic I felt.

My father was approaching us across the water. He tethered his little boat and we hugged again. Finally, we were reunited.

He picked up the bags at our feet. I held Asteri under my arm, and the three of us climbed into the boat. Nikos held tightly onto my hand as we left the island behind for ever.

I looked back at Spinalonga and then at Nikos. In a single moment, I had found both love and freedom.

HALFWAY BETWEEN SPINALONGA AND PLAKA, with water lapping gently around us and the sound of the engine almost drowning my voice, I told my father our news. He had met Doctor Kyritsis several times when he returned from the island and they had even had coffee together. My father could not have been happier.

Dimitris was waiting by the quay in Plaka when we got there. I told him too that Doctor Kyritsis and I were to be married. He hugged me tightly.

"I am so happy for you, Maria," he said, beaming. "But we will still write to each other?"

Dimitris was to leave for Athens, where he had been offered a place to study mathematics at university.

"Of course," I promised him. "Just as we used to!"

There was a big celebration in Plaka that night, with music and dancing and a huge feast that the villagers of Plaka provided. The party went on until very late.

In the following days everyone went their separate ways.

FOR MANY YEARS AFTERWARDS, NOW THAT the cure for leprosy had been found, Nikos and I travelled together all round the world. I had never left Crete before but we soon went to India, Nigeria and Brazil, treating people and taking medicine to cure them. They were exciting years.

We also began to do surgery for the eyes, hands and feet to alleviate some of the damage caused by this disease.

We told people we met the truth: that leprosy is a matter of bad luck, not a punishment from God. When they heard the story of Spinalonga and our community there and saw that I lived without shame, it gave them courage.

In many places, the shame and stigma of leprosy finally began to lift. For a long time, people found it hard to accept that it is a disease like any other which is spread with bacteria and is now completely curable!

Some people never changed their views, however. Anna never invited us to her home and, since the day she noticed the mark on my leg, I have not seen my niece.

Dimitris became a professor in Athens, got married and now has fifteen grandchildren. We still write letters every month.

Nikos and I had our precious daughter and we continued to travel together even after she was born. Finally, when we retired, we moved back to Crete.

"And of course, Nikos was your grandfather and our daughter is your mother!" says Yiayia, as she finishes telling the story.

I feel so proud to think that my grandmother lived through all this and survived. I am so glad she has told me her story. Perhaps the shame of leprosy stayed a little too long, even with her.

I also understand now why she wants to stay in this place, with all these memories.

"We always knew that this was home. And for me it always will be," she says quietly.

She takes my hand and leads me down to the water's edge so that I can see Spinalonga more clearly. I can imagine her waving to her mother all those years before and I can make out the hospital and the house where she and Dimitris lived.

I have so many questions, but before I ask them it is time to return to Agios Nikolaos. We haven't even dipped our toes in the sea but the bus is coming down the hill and we have to catch it.

On the bus, there is something I need to ask her. What did she mean when she told my mother that she has "too much to look after" to leave Crete?

"That's simple," she says. "I go over to Spinalonga once a year to tend my mother's grave."

In Greece this is a very important thing to do, so now I understand why she will always live here, a short journey away from Spinalonga.

When we get back to the apartment, Yiayia says there is something she wants to show me. Delving into the back of a cupboard, she pulls out a tatty scrapbook and passes it to me. I sit in her old armchair and begin to turn the pages. They are her mother's – my great-grandmother's – drawings of Spinalonga. The pictures are even more beautiful than I had imagined.

Yiayia sits down beside me and I notice she has something in her hands. It is the paperweight, the stone she painted for her mother. It was taken to Spinalonga but now lives on the dresser and I remember dusting it that morning. She holds it out to me.

"Look," she says, smiling. "It's your Greek lesson for today. It says: Kathe mera tha se skefto.*"*

I take it from her hands, remembering what she and her mother promised each other all those years before. It was a promise they never broke.

"Every day I will think of you."

LEPROSY IN THE 21ST CENTURY

Leprosy is one of the world's oldest diseases. It is caused by a bacteria that affects the nerves of the hands, feet and face. If left untreated it can cause pain, disfigurement and result in permanent disability. There is now an effective cure, but millions of people around the world are still disabled by the consequences of leprosy and are subjected to discrimination and social exclusion, like Eleni, Dimitris and Maria in the story. This prejudice also makes people fearful of coming forward for diagnosis.

VICTORIA HISLOP IS AN AMBASSADOR FOR LEPRA

As the world's first leprosy prevention organisation, Lepra is an international charity that has been at the forefront of prevention, treatment and management of leprosy since 1924. The charity works directly with those affected in Bangladesh, India, Mozambique and Zimbabwe, across which two thirds of the world's cases occur. Beyond ensuring health needs are met, they fight prejudice by amplifying the voices of those affected by leprosy, supporting people to improve their lives and livelihoods and campaigning to keep people with their communities rather than in colonies or isolation, as happened on Spinalonga.

If you are able, there are two ways you could support Lepra. Firstly, you could make a donation today, for example £20 will train one village doctor to recognise the symptoms of leprosy; this is vital to ensure an accurate diagnosis and guarantee that people are given the correct treatment as soon as possible. Secondly, you could support Lepra by getting involved in their schools fundraising programme, and encourage students and school teachers to participate. For more information, please go to lepra.org.uk/get-involved/fundraise/schools-and-young-people.

- Make a donation online with a credit card, debit card or PayPal at lepra.org.uk
- Call Lepra on 01206 216700
- Text LEPRA followed by your donation amount to 70500
- Send a cheque to Lepra, 28 Middleborough, Colchester, Essex CO1 1TG

We will beat
leprosy together